THE MIRROR & THE MONKEY

by

R. S. Deese

with

illustrations by Chuck Wadey

The Mirror & The Monkey by R. S. Deese
with illustrations by Chuck Wadey

ISBN: 978-1-949790-53-5 (pbk)
ISBN: 978-1-949790-55-9 (hbk)
ISBN: 978-1-949790-54-2 (ebk)

Layout by Mark Givens

First Pelekinesis Printing 2022

For information:

Pelekinesis, 112 Harvard Ave #65, Claremont, CA 91711 USA

Library of Congress Cataloging-in-Publication Data

Names: Deese, R. S., 1964- author.
Title: The mirror & the monkey / by R.S. Deese ; with illustrations by
   Chuck Wadey.
Other titles: Mirror and the monkey
Description: Claremont, CA : Pelekinesis, 2022. | Summary: "A king who
   seeks to keep his kingdom safe and immaculate orders the destruction of
   a flower that he regards as pernicious weed, but soon finds that he has
   awakened the dragon who sleeps beneath a nearby mountain. The dragon
   takes her revenge on the king by eating his favorite horse and turning
   his firstborn son into a monkey. The king's angry reaction to this sets
   in motion a chain of events that will destroy his kingdom and scatter
   its people in all directions. In the midst of these events the young
   monkey will discover the pain of loss, the joy of love, and the secret
   of who he is"-- Provided by publisher.
Identifiers: LCCN 2021029581 (print) | LCCN 2021029582 (ebook) | ISBN
   9781949790535 (trade paperback) | ISBN 9781949790559 (hardcover) |
   ISBN
   9781949790542 (epub)
Classification: LCC PS3604.E2995 M57 2022 (print) | LCC PS3604.E2995
   (ebook) | DDC 813/.6--dc23
LC record available at https://lccn.loc.gov/2021029581
LC ebook record available at https://lccn.loc.gov/2021029582

www.pelekinesis.com

The Mirror

&

The Monkey

by

R. S. Deese

with illustrations by
Chuck Wadey

To the memory of Howard Drucker, revered friend and storyteller.

"Lifetime is a child at play, moving pieces in a game. Kingship belongs to the child."

Heraclitus
Fragments, XCIV

After tonight, in accordance with the King's command, the Monkey will never have existed. The tall man raises the King's bow and draws his arrow back with some difficulty. The fat man struggles to hold the black silk bag at arm's length, as the monkey slips around inside it. He takes a deep breath and whispers to the tall man that something might be moving through the underbrush. The tall man glares at him. He clears his throat and spits, then lets the arrow fly.

The Monkey has closed his eyes and reckoned the flight of the arrow. Before it can come to cleave his heart, it will have to fly across the meadow, and before it can fly across the meadow, it must fly halfway across. And before it flies halfway to that point... On the edge of a second that splits itself unendingly into fragments of a second, each of them still made of precious time, the Monkey sees eternity. He curls in on himself like a child about to be born, and he begins to dream.

THE LION'S TOOTH

A subtle foot of curling root
A stalk sewn equal to the breeze
A wreath of lion's tooth to boot

Now greet the lowly eye that sees
A mirror of the sun & moon
Between the shadows of the trees

This humble flower is the one
The blind of heart still call a weed
One empire cracked and scores begun

By the flight of a single seed

Once, in a time so long ago that only the rocks can remember it now, when the world was one island surrounded by one sea, there grew a single dandelion on the shoulder of a great black mountain, beside a creek of vanishing snow. When it was young, its petals spread out like rays of light. The ants crawling up a nearby rock thought they saw a second sun in the sky above.

One night, the ants looked to the flower and saw a sphere that glowed with a gray light. They thought they saw a second moon in the sky above, until a wind came down the mountainside and blew the sphere apart. A generation of dandelion seeds floated through the air, and they began to perish. Some were caught on the blades of grass that grew beside the creek, while others touched the water's surface and were swept away.

One seed made it across the stream and past the eyes of a frog, who knew that it was not a bug because it made no sound. It drifted over the smooth rocks along the creek and between the leafless branches of a fallen tree, until it was caught in the lacing of a spider web. The maker of the web crawled out to see the seed as it trembled in the breeze. She decided it was not to eat and went back to her weaving. Soon, a hungry old crow swept down from the sky to eat the spider in a single snap. The bird took flight again with a shred of spider web still clinging to his foot, and at the end of one silk thread dangled the small seed.

Still on the hunt for things to eat, the crow rose higher and higher and turned out toward the marshes. A crosswind broke the strand of thread. Swept by a strong current in the sky, the seed flew far across the island of the world, over deserts, forests, lakes, and foothills, and past the smoldering mountain where the Dragon slept, until it passed through the high and thorny crest that lined the outer wall of the kingdom of Kósomos, which the king bragged was home to every man, woman, and child on earth (save a single wily girl said to roam the wilderness).

The seed flew over the fertile smelling pens where King Urikiru, the founder and protector of Kósomos, kept his elephants, pigs, and sheep. It passed across another wall and drifted through the rising scents of jasmine and citrus flowers and above rows of broad grape leaves that glistened in the sun. Finally, it crossed the wall of the city itself and floated above the fine stone houses that lined a network of orderly streets, laid out in nine concentric rings and cut by nine broad boulevards reaching outward from the Palace. The granite stones that paved the Palace court were locked together in a magnificent pattern and scrubbed as clean as the bronze dish from which the King liked to eat his roasted birds, buttered snails, fried plantains, and fresh hibiscus flowers each night. It was here in the center of the city that the seed now made its home, in a dark and tiny gap between two spotless paving stones.

THE QUEEN

The dreamer she weaves in her womb
Weaves her into the same dream
Neither knowing who nor whom

Knowing neither be nor seem
Only an illicit thought
That lights creation with its gleam:

One white seed floating from without
Three walls the King built high and strong
To settle in a sweet, dark spot

Where it does not belong

In the center of Kósomos, as they lay beside each other on the little green island in the middle of a cool dark sea beneath the starry ceiling of the Palace Dome, the King and Queen were each secluded in their dreams. Queen Ambu, whose belly had grown for close to nine cycles of the moon, was now a brilliant fish who swam in wide circles around the island of the world. She swam through towering forests of kelp, over twisted reefs whose colors she could not name and whose existence she would never have suspected, and through dim red caverns that were gateways to the sea of fire that ebbs and flows beneath the world. Drawn upward by a shifting beam of light, she came near the water's surface and meandered through a shallow tide pool by the shore, studying the erratic traffic of the crabs and the cool undulations of the sea anemones beneath her.

It was not long before the King, who sought to bring every good and beautiful thing into his Kingdom, came galloping along the seashore on his mighty horse Kalypso, a white mare with a deep black crescent on her back. He stopped to admire this beautiful fish as its scales shot back the noonday sun. "I am building the world again inside my Palace Dome," he told his horse, "and this fish shall be a part of it." He caught her in his drinking cup and brought her back to the cool dark sea that surrounded the little green Island of the World inside his Palace Dome.

Kalypso snorted and neighed, then asked the King, with a piercing glare, if this was a *true* model of the world that he had created inside his Palace Dome.

"Yes," the King replied.

Then how could it be, the horse whinnied, that the Island of the World inside his Palace Dome had no magnificent kingdom of Kósomos with three high walls, nine broad boulevards, and a great white Palace Dome upon it?

Urikiru was startled by this question, which could only be answered with deeds. He set to work to build just such a kingdom on his little island. At the center of this kingdom was the Palace Dome, but this begged the question, Kalypso averred, of just what was inside *it*. Clearly the King's work was far from finished, but he would not be caught shirking—especially by his favorite horse. Each new dome had a tinier sea within it and required a tinier fish to swim around its little green island. And every time, Queen Ambu discovered—she was that fish.

As her mind swam through each shrinking moat, she turned in her sleep and prayed for some outside force, whatever it might be, to break the logic of this dream. A tiny noise tickled the inside of her ear, and she dreamt about the flight of the seed, drifting in its lazy path over the high and thorny walls surrounding the city.

THE KING

Half asleep, the old man muses:
If only I were one with my horse
—A centaur beats a king for most uses—

I'd leave my kingdom (with a force
Of guards to guard it) and taste the air
Outside these walls, then fill my purse

With fat red berries from up there
Where steam breaks from the mountainside
You cannot get such berries here

No thought would break my stride

The King's dreams always began well enough. On many
nights, as he settled into sleep, Urikiru would imagine that
his body, from just below his navel down, was the body of his
mighty mare, Kalypso. This thought, which he could share with

no one, filled him with unspeakable delight. He felt the sun fall on his muscular shoulders and arms, and he looked down to admire his four strong legs, his lean flanks, and the deep black crescent on his back. The King saw that his Kingdom was clean and in good order, so he supposed that he could leave it with his guards for a short time.

He headed toward the outer gate of Kósomos, his eye on the forest, still wet with that morning's rain, and on the smoldering black mountain beyond. As he galloped through the gate, a taught wire—so thin it was invisible— caught him just below his navel and sliced his body clean in two without slowing the horse's stride. Urikiru touched his open torso as a warm puddle the color of wine grew all around him, and the headless body of Kalypso fled into the wilderness.

As the King's blood flowed away, he saw the world he had built transformed at once into a blighted ruin. The gates were broken open to the wind, the people lost to the wilds beyond, and spangled shards of the Palace Dome lay scattered all around the plaza as though it had exploded from within. Wild boars feasted in the granaries while dirty blond apes with curious paws and flaring red rumps roamed the streets squeaking songs to each other that were at once mysterious and obscene to the august old ear of the King. Even the paving stones in his plaza, which all fit together in a magnificent pattern and were scrubbed each night by his palace guards, were now being cracked and pushed apart by a promiscuous crop of weeds, with yellow flowers and broad jagged leaves, that blew in from the wilderness.

Wiping the sweat from his face, Urikiru sat up. The sky was still dark outside the Palace windows and the birds were silent in the trees. He reached down and touched his legs, happy to find that they were still there. He kissed Queen Ambu as she slept beside him, and took a long moment to study her face, which, though it had been troubled while he was sleeping, was now graced by a serene smile. Her long black hair fell over her ripe growing breasts and the taut dome of her belly moved as her child moved within.

The King now raised his eyes to admire the high and intricate dome of lapis tile above their heads and the gilded stars that shimmered in the dancing light of the water beneath. He climbed into his little boat and rowed across the cool dark sea to inspect the Kingdom he had built.

Urikiru stood upon the balcony that surrounded his Palace dome. Tonight the moon was full and he could see his whole creation in its light. He studied the concentric streets that he had traced himself, and the perfectly straight boulevards that stretched outward from his plaza like rays of sunlight. He looked far beyond the city walls, at the black mountain range that looked to his fond eyes like a reclining woman with a shapely belly and two ample breasts. He listened to the distant roar of last winter's snow as it rushed into the sluices of his aqueduct. The streets were immaculate, the trees were pruned, and the mangos in the grove beyond the inner wall were ready to be harvested. The animals were all content and asleep in their pens, and the citizens were all content and asleep in their beds.

Then Urikiru saw something that made him gnaw his lower lip so hard he tasted his own blood. In the center of his unblemished Kingdom, he saw what he had seen in his dream: a spindly yellow flower surrounded by a bush of saw-tooth leaves grown up between two paving stones. He felt his legs buckle beneath him and the drops of sweat return to his forehead as he rang the old iron bell to call his soldiers to the Palace. Queen Ambu awakened. She dove into the cool dark sea and swam across it. Then she put on her blue silk gown and went out to the balcony to stand at Urikiru's side and see just what the matter was.

Queen Ambu's eyes were so sharp that even from the balcony, she could admire the flower's deep yellow hue, the jagged splendor of its leaves, and the sheer courage it had shown in rooting where it did. She remembered the floating seed from her dream and advised Urikiru to leave the flower alone. He would not listen to her, so she sighed and went back to bed. The King commanded his soldiers to surround the dandelion, rip it up by the roots and burn it on the spot. Sleepy though they were, they grumbled and jostled with each other so that each of them could play a part, however small, in protecting the Kingdom of Kósomos. The flower was uprooted, and the soldiers lined up so they could each whack it with the shovel blade before they set it afire. After the men had fulfilled Urikiru's command, the King shouted at them from the balcony.

"Each of you was born within the safety of Kósomos. Your memories are full of fond and feeble things, and so you can't imagine what these high walls shield you from: the darkness that hides in the bark of the trees and then floods the whole forest when the sun goes down, the nettles that would cut your flesh with every step you take, the flying, buzzing parasites that can undo your sanity before they take your blood and leave you with the gift of their disease, the yellow eyed cats that roam the wild mango groves. They are beautiful to look at, and they nuzzle your belly at first the way a kitten does, but then they open up their teeth and lap your blood and guts the way a kitten laps its bowl of cream!"

Urikiru thought that the last part about the cats was especially frightening, so he was appalled to hear one of his soldiers titter once and bite his tongue, though the King couldn't see in the darkness just who it was. And so, he recited his speech two more times—with some kingly refinements—as his men stood at attention, dressed in their full battle armor, and shifted their weight on their tired legs. When at last he was finished with his solemn address, Urikiru listened for a long minute to the grave silence of his loyal men, then sent them back to their quarters.

Before the King went back to sleep, he kissed Queen Ambu's belly and whispered, as he had each night for nine cycles of the moon, "Hello, my Prince" into her navel. As the Queen sighed and shifted in her sleep, King Urikiru recited the long tale of his Kingdom. "It began with the first wall: a simple circle of stones around a small fire to save it from the wind. Now I have built three strong walls and every good and useful thing that feeds the fire of civilization is safe within these high stone walls, and every odd pernicious thing is locked without. Kósomos completes the world. The snowflakes from the sky gather on the mountainside and wait for the spring sun to melt them so they may flow into the channels of our aqueduct and become the very blood of our kingdom, the sweet black grapes that grow in our vineyards are swollen with joy and ache for the touch of the girl's foot that will press them into wine, and the tall magnolia trees that line our well-kept streets each springtime give their fragrance to the breeze as a gift made from their gratitude, for here they are watered, pruned and guarded from the blights and winds that rattle through the wilderness. This is the Kingdom that you will inherit. As the first wall saved the fire from the wind, you will keep the people safe and spare them from destruction."

Urikiru now thought again of the faceless soldier who had snickered at his speech. A frown tightened his sunburned face, and he tasted the blood on his cut lip. "My son, the King is the loneliest man on earth. His enemies are great and small, and no one thanks him well enough for the work he does."

While Urikiru and Ambu slept, the smoke from the scorched dandelion floated far beyond the walls of the Kingdom. It drifted up the side of the black mountain, passed over strange and misshapen rocks, and slipped into the blind and bottomless cave where the Dragon was sleeping. The faintest wisp of dandelion smoke curled in the Dragon's nostrils and entered the kingdom of her dreams.

At dawn, when Urikiru and Ambu were happily sharing a dreamless sleep, they were shocked awake by an earthquake that rocked the Palace so violently some stars fell from the dome of heaven and splashed into the cool dark sea around the Island of the World. The King hurried to the balcony and looked up at the mountain range. Its shapely form trembled with such force that ancient trees now snapped and fell and turned their roots up to the sun, and boulders that had not moved for centuries came tumbling down the mountainside.

Soon, a colossal serpent broke the mountain open like a child that kills its mother in the act of being born. The Dragon walked on two legs like the King himself, and her long tail was jagged like the leaves of the flower that had invaded the Kingdom of Kósomos. She snapped trees with a whip of her tail, and the whole valley creaked with every step she took. When the Dragon arrived at the edge of the city, she could smell the King's stables. She smashed her tail into the outer wall to knock it down and feed her hunger. She chose Kalypso, the powerful white mare with a deep black crescent on her back and embraced her with her tongue and teeth. She let the great creature struggle for a while in her mouth, before crushing her to savor the fear and desperation that now seasoned her blood. Urikiru rang the old iron bell again to call his troops to battle, then grabbed his hunting bow and quiver of arrows and headed for the breech in the wall. The Dragon stood and licked her teeth and waited for him.

The King was so possessed with rage that he did not think to put his clothes or armor on. As he marched across the plaza, naked and ready to do battle with the dragon, he was stopped by Skalyya, the secretive Priest of the Kingdom, who was many years older than the King. He collected ancient superstitions and kept an ear on the sounds of the wilderness beyond the city walls. The Priest was short and fat, with eyes as gloomy and opaque as the immaculate black robe that always concealed his soft white hands. He didn't show his face much around the Palace, but on certain nights he moved like a wild boar through the underbrush of the King's dreams. Urikiru never took Skalyya's counsel, but he knew that the Priest's influence was wide among the people of Kósomos, and that some of his own warriors had, against the King's stern admonitions, gone to the old man for cures, spells, and befuddling notions. Now Skalyya stood in the King's path and looked up at him with his rheumy eyes.

"Go home," said the Priest. "You may be clever and good with weapons, but I have wrestled with the Dragon ten thousand times in my sleep and cogitations before you were even born to walk this earth. Believe me, this one has powers that your mind is too small to dream of."

King Urikiru, who never put much stock in magic or spells or anything the Priest had to say, ignored the old man's warning and continued on his way. Skalyya shouted from behind him, "You would be wise not to look in her eyes." Though he pretended not the hear him, these words burned in Urikiru's ears and he felt at once that, in spite of his proper contempt for the Priest, he would take his advice on this one point.

When he arrived at the breech in the wall, the King found his troops huddled together behind the pigpens. He borrowed a sword from one of his frightened men, strode forward and swung it at the giant beast as calmly as if buttering a snail that he was about to eat. The Dragon was huge and powerful, but Urikiru was brave and nimble, and soon he exhausted the giant beast the way a darting housefly can exhaust the one who tries to swat it. When the Dragon was short of breath, Urikiru charged and sliced off the tip of her tail. It slithered in the grass like a headless snake, and two of the braver soldiers chased it with their swords and wrestled with it on the ground, which made the others laugh and helped them to forget their fear.

Now painted with the Dragon's blood, the King laughed like a red demon to see the Dragon rattled and weakened just a little. Determined not to waste this moment, he grabbed a spear from one of the soldiers and drove it straight through her left foot. When the Dragon doubled over in pain, King Urikiru wrapped an oily rag around the tip of an arrow, set it afire, and shot it. Though he did not dare look at his target, Urikiru reckoned his arc with precision and sent the flaming arrow deep into the Dragon's right eye. Her painful wail and her thunderous fall sent a ring of low vibrations through the valley and signaled the King's triumph. As the Dragon lay paralyzed with pain, King Urikiru shouted to his men, "A scar is the surest form of memory!" and unsheathed his obsidian dagger. This was the King's oldest weapon—the one he had made to slay his enemies and skin great beasts in the forest, long before the founding of Kósomos. Now he carved the mark of Kósomos, a bow and arrow (or was it a bird in flight?) with three strokes of his obsidian dagger upon the heaving flesh of her right flank. Then, like a calf that suckles at the teat of its mother, Urikiru drank the Dragon's blood from the wound he had made. The King strode back to his men, his smiling face now red with Dragon's blood, as they greeted him with an awful burst of whistles, yells, and undulating battle cries. With her remaining eye, the wounded creature looked back once at the city of Kósomos, casting a long and steady glance into the eyes of Queen Ambu, who watched her from the balcony of the Palace Dome. Then the Dragon turned back to the wild. She lifted her colossal body up and crawled toward her mountain cave, a wide trail of blood streaming from her foot and tail, and a halo of magnificent griffon vultures circling above her.

As the wounded Dragon burrowed back into her hole, the earth shook again and an avalanche of rocks closed her smoking cave behind her. When the dust settled and the last echoes of the Dragon's cries faded in the distance, the King looked up and admired the shapely mountain again.

"The monster is no more!" King Urikiru declared. "I left her *just* enough strength to crawl back into her hole and die. Why should we be troubled to dig her grave when she can do it for herself?" The soldiers laughed and hoisted the King upon their shoulders. They carried him to the tavern where they drank barrels of deep red wine and reenacted the battle a dozen times. The King played himself, and scores of soldiers climbed all over each other to play the giant, hapless Dragon. The raucous celebration lasted long enough for the moon to pass its zenith and begin to descend, while Skalyya sat silently in his cloister and watched and waited.

As the soldiers drank more and more wine, the King ran his tongue over his chops and tasted the traces of Dragon blood. It had a bitter and bracing taste that lit a strange fire in the center of his chest and made his old eyes glow again. As he touched the hilt of the obsidian dagger he had used that day to carve his mark into the Dragon's flank, the King felt a new and restless power move within the circuit of his blood.

THE MONKEY

A man who dreams he is a monkey
Who dreams he is a fish, and a fish
Who dreams she is a dreaming monkey

Who dreams a man but wakes a fish
Are all the same while the fish is awake
And the man still slumbers in his wish

What difference, really, does it make
Who is a fish, a monkey, or a man?
None but this: the world will break

To wake the sleeping man

As the moon fell beneath the outer wall of the Kingdom and cast the shadow of its thorny crest on the immense white dome of the Palace, Urikiru came back home to find that Queen Ambu had given birth to a monkey. He let out a high laugh at first, thinking it was some kind of drunken dream, as he saw the Queen hold the monkey to her breast and let him play with the hem of her blue silk gown. She caressed the dark hair on his back and called him Ololo, or "Prince" in a tongue more ancient than the city of Kósomos. She brought him near the window, so he could hear the congress of the passerine birds singing throughout the forest. Ambu spoke the language of the birds, which was lost to everyone else in the city, and she poured its sounds into his ear in a stream of whispers warm as mother's milk: "Listen to the birds, Ololo. They fly farther in a day than any man or beast walks in a lifetime. Their songs will teach you all about the deserts, forests, lakes, and mountains, and the great sea that surrounds them all." As if to answer her, the child wrapped his tiny red hand around her little finger and let out a luxurious sigh.

As Urikiru came closer, he had no more room to doubt that it really was a monkey who greedily drank warm milk from Queen Ambu's breast. The King became frightened for a moment, but soon he felt an invincible rage rising from his gut to his chest and pulsing through his arms. He grabbed the Queen by the throat and accused her of sneaking out beyond the high walls of Kósomos. "It was you who planted that dirty little weed inside my Kingdom! And now I see that you have opened your womb to the filthy seed of some ape out in the jungle!"

Ambu laughed at his wild accusations and implored the King to look at Ololo. "His eyes are yours! Look at him move and hear the music that he speaks. He has your wit and speed. And when I hold him to my breast, he has your touch and tenderness!" The King could not bear to look at the Monkey, but Ololo saw the King's white hair, broad shoulders and blood-stained body and thought he was magnificent. It was only when the King drew his obsidian dagger that Ololo learned to fear him. Now he held the dagger by the tip of its blade and cocked his arm behind his head, ready to send it flying. The Monkey leapt in a panic and darted from left to right but, with every move he made, the King's eyes followed him. When the Monkey froze in fear with an open window at his back, the King sent his dagger flying. Queen Ambu locked her eyes on the dagger and it stopped in midair, just so long as she kept her eyes upon it. She stepped in front of her child and stood in the path of the dagger. "If you would touch a single hair on his back, you will have to kill me first!" Then she raised her eyes to look directly into the King's and the dagger resumed its flight, piercing her flesh and finding its home in her heart.

She kept her eyes locked on the King's as her body fell

backwards out the Palace window. Queen Ambu tumbled down the Palace wall and landed in the same spot where the yellow flower had grown the day before. Three of the King's soldiers, still drunk with wine, had lingered in the plaza to sing songs about the glories of that day's battle. When they saw what the King had done, they cried out in horror. Urikiru stood on the balcony and looked down at them. For a long moment he said nothing, for all the words he knew had fled his mind in fear. But then the rage rose in his chest again and his voice boomed with anger even as it cracked with grief. He ordered them to take the Queen away and cast her body in the dank stone vaults deep below the city, where not a soul would see it. "Be sure to scrub the paving stones before the sun is up!"

Each of the three soldiers took off his dark wool cape, and together they made shroud that they wrapped with great care around the Queen, concealing her and absorbing the blood from her mortal wound. Then they scrubbed the ground as best they could, even as their tears fell and mingled with Queen Ambu's blood. As hard as they tried, they could not remove the deep red stain in the space between the paving stones. The King told them that the work they had done was good enough and sent them deep below the city to leave Queen Ambu's body there. He praised them all as loyal soldiers, then locked the gate behind them and waited for the pale tribe of alligators that lived beneath the city to do its work. As he heard the screams of the three soldiers echo upward through the chasm of his privy and then disappear, the King stood up and emptied his bladder, then licked his chops again to taste the lingering traces of Dragon's blood. This had been no accident, the King surmised, but only what was necessary. He was right to kill the faithless Queen Ambu and the traitors who had mourned for her. Now he would kill the Monkey. He could hear the little beast weeping and followed the sound of his sobs as they echoed through the Palace.

Ololo saw the King come after him and grabbed onto the sunburst chandelier that hung from the center of the Palace Dome. Everything within the King's reach, from saucers to bowls to torches mounted on the wall, was suddenly a weapon to be hurled at the hated thing. The Monkey was agile, dodging every missile large and small, flaming or sharp, that came his way. Leaping high and low and here and there, the Monkey exhausted the King, just as the King had used his wiles to deplete the strength of the Dragon. Short of breath, but driven by an unstoppable rage, the King chased the Monkey through every room in the Palace, from the deepest basements to the highest parapets, but the agile Ololo was always just beyond his reach.

Finally, the King called on his two most trusted confidants: Thorn, the tall assassin who knew ten thousand ways to kill, and Rakelvor, the man with fat hands and a baby face who knew just how to keep a secret. The two men arrived without delay, and the King gave them their payment in advance. To Rakelvor he gave his gold medallion, which bore a portrait of the King floating on a cloud with his bow and quiver of arrows on one face, and a map of Kósomos on the other. To Thorn he gave his golden hunting bow and quiver of twelve golden arrows.

Thorn and Rakelvor were so astounded by these gifts that they did not dare to speak. The King's eyes seemed to look straight through them and far into the distance as he said, "A wicked monkey from beyond the city walls has invaded this Palace. You two will catch it, take it far into the wilderness whence it came, and make it disappear forever. And then, you will never speak a word of it, on pain of death." And with those words the King went to his private chamber, determined to never think of the Monkey again.

Thorn and Rakelvor set out to catch the Monkey. From the basement to the parapets, their luck was hardly better than the King's had been. Twice Ololo stood still long enough for Rakelvor to lunge at him, and twice the Monkey leapt straight into the air and let the ample Secretary fall face first to the floor. Thorn watched Ololo's games with some amusement until they came to the cool dark sea that surrounded the Island of the World. At the edge of the little sea, the Monkey caught sight of his own reflection, then squeaked and ran away in fear. The Assassin called the exhausted Secretary to his side and whispered in his ear. As Rakelvor wiped his brow and let out a mischievous giggle, Thorn took a mirror down from the wall and slowly walked toward Ololo with it. Terrified at the sight of the Monkey in the glass, Ololo turned and ran again—straight into the darkness of Rakelvor's black silk bag.

Their prisoner was now in hand, and so Thorn and Rakelvor marched off into the night to earn their pay.

THE ASSASSIN & THE SECRETARY

Every kingdom since the first
That brought the wild to order
From the finest to the worst

Folds lies into its charter
And spills the blood of innocents
As lime into its mortar

To bind great stones into a fence
A king must guard the art of killing
And gather jewels of high expense

As honors for the willing

As Thorn and Rakelvor marched miles and miles
into the wilderness, far from the glow of the city, Rakelvor
whistled tunelessly while Thorn sang a song to guard against
the loneliness that assassins sometimes feel. Though each of

them had committed, or quietly arranged, scores of murders for one good reason or another, they had spent their lives in the confines of the city and were both a little scared of the darkness that seemed to know no limit beyond its walls.

Though they did not know it, the Assassin and the Secretary were not alone. A wily girl named Tahualamne, who had lived by her wits in the woods all her life, followed Thorn and Rakelvor through the night as they discussed how  best to kill the Monkey. She could hear Ololo's muffled squeaks as he struggled to escape from the sack. She spoke a few words to Ololo in the language of the birds, and he answered her in kind. If the Assassin and the Secretary heard these sounds, they did not know their meaning and thought nothing of them.

When Thorn determined that they'd gone far enough, he ordered Rakelvor to hold the bag up at arm's length. Rakelvor thought he heard something moving in the underbrush, but Thorn glared at him to keep quiet. The Assassin steadied his footing and flattened his bloodless lips. Drawing back the bow with some difficulty, he cleared his throat and spat on the ground, then closed one eye and took aim with his arrow.

Tahualamne now slipped through the grass and laced a long and thorny vine around Rakelvor's ankles, so gently that he did not hear or feel a thing. When she saw Thorn spit and let his arrow fly, she closed the figure eight, and Rakelvor screamed out in pain and fell down on his knees. Ololo leapt out of the bag just in time to see Thorn's first arrow slice through Rakelvor's neck and nail him to the trunk of the tree.

As Rakelvor gasped and began to drown in his own blood, Ololo unclasped the gold medallion from his neck, used his wide head as a step to climb up into the high branches of the tree. Thorn fired relentlessly at the Monkey, studding the tree with golden arrows as he missed the Monkey every time. When Thorn had shot all his arrows, Ololo quietly collected them. He then leapt from the darkness onto the Assassin's back, pressed the razor tip of an arrow against his neck and gently took away his bow. Like a wise soldier who knows when to retreat, Thorn ran back toward the city. Admiring his new medallion and bow, the Monkey was happy to let him escape.

But it was not to be. A pair of hungry tigers who had picked up the scent of the fat man nailed to the tree found the defenseless Thorn and tore his lean body in half in a lazy bout of tug-of-war. When every scrap that they could eat of lean and lanky Thorn was gone, the cats came to the tree and feasted for nearly an hour on the bountiful flesh of Rakelvor. Then the tigers curled up together at the base of the tree and fell asleep.

Ololo watched the tigers sleep and thought about his bare escape. He remembered bits of birdsong he had heard when he was being carried to his execution, and he wondered who had saved his life. He studied the bloodstained grass beneath him, and he found the thorny vine wound neatly in a figure eight around the wet bones of Rakelvor's ankles. He looked in every direction, but Tahualamne had vanished in the underbrush the way a shining minnow darts into the darkness of the sea. Ololo looked up and swore to the sky, in the language of the birds, that he would find her.

But, for now, he did not dare to climb down from this tree. He felt hungry and cold as he sat in its low branches and looked down at the sleeping tigers. Their bellies rose and fell in a slow and easy rhythm that made Ololo close his eyes and remember his mother's breath as he laid his head against her breast. Drifting into sleep, he was like an ancient sailor who drew his whole life from the sea and was grateful for its gentle rhythm as it buoyed his little boat.

The smaller tiger shifted in the grass. She opened her eyes, looked up and at him and bared her brilliant teeth. Her low roar rattled the Monkey's bones and awakened her companion. Ololo knew he had to escape. He climbed up the branches of the tree and broke through the leaves to find himself beneath a shocking canopy of stars. He could not touch them, but he could touch the gold medallion that glowed with their light. He also touched the sharp tips of his arrows and fingered the taut string of his bow. These objects felt strange at first to his fingers and toes, but he would quickly learn how to use them well.

Hearing the tigers circle and hiss beneath his tree, the Monkey leapt to another tree until the tigers prowled around the base of that one, and then he leapt to the next and next, panicked at how fast the cats could move. Soon the Monkey was leaping so fast from tree to tree that he felt like he was flying. He kept his eyes on the stars above, sparing no time to look at the tigers below.

THE PRIEST

Important lies ought never go
Out poor & naked. They must glisten
In the half light with the glow

Of miracles. Every ear will listen
To the music of a lie well told
As every eye will fasten

On a bird that takes its baths in gold.
And baffled folk should never sing, except to sing *along*
Their minds must never be as bold

As their bones are strong

Back at the Palace, the King sat alone and stared at the floor, waiting for Thorn and Rakelvor. Hours before he had been triumphant: He had drawn the Dragon's blood and sent the beast back to her mountain cave to die alone. He had reminded his soldiers, who had lived too long without the sight of combat, what courage was, and he had been drunk and bloody and full of pride as he came home to see the son his Queen had given him. That little beast!

Tonight, he had no Queen, no heir, and now it seemed that his deadliest Assassin and most trusted Secretary had vanished in the wilderness. He dreamt about the obsidian knife with which he'd killed his loving Queen, and wished he still had the blade to cleave his own heart.

The King wept.

On the other side of the city and in his secret hovel, Skalyya closed his eyes and whispered a solemn priestly prayer as he listened to the King's cries of guilt and despair. He snipped off a few grizzled hairs from his chin and mixed them in a golden bowl with his own blood and tears, three dozen pair of firefly wings, and a vial of phosphorous that he had distilled from his own secretions.

In the middle of the night there was a knock at the King's chamber door. When Urikiru opened the door, he saw neither Thorn nor Rakelvor, but the living, breathing image of Queen Ambu. Urikiru fell down on his knees and begged for her forgiveness. The Queen that he saw before him smiled silently and caressed his head, for she bore no scars and had no memory at all of the King's offense.

"She is my miracle," said Skalyya, "She will never be cross with you, for she has lost the will to speak. I am the one to whom you must listen if you would learn where and how to find forgiveness. If you had heeded my warning, you would have never lost your Queen and you would have an heir to rule your Kingdom. I brought Queen Ambu back to you to show you that my craft is real. If you take my counsel now, I can show you how to make *peace* with the Dragon who lives inside the mountain, so that you may have an heir."

Urikiru bowed his head. From behind his dark black cloak, Skalyya extended his pale blue hand, which King Urikiru had never seen before. The King was shocked at how cold it felt but still he humbly lowered his face to kiss the old Priest's knuckles. "I will do whatever you say."

To which Skalyya replied, "This is a debt that must be paid in blood." He gave elaborate instructions to the King, which Urikiru had his soldiers carry out with neither deviation nor delay. They went to every household in the Kingdom and collected a tax of ten paving stones from every floor, and all the gold and precious stones that they could find inside the people's homes.

Under Skalyya's exacting command, the soldiers brought the massive stones and brilliant jewels to the center of the plaza and began to build a magnificent altar. The Priest declared that it would be twice as tall as the King's Palace and shimmer so brightly beneath the moon that all the roosters of the kingdom would sing to it at midnight as though it were the light of dawn.

When the people of the Kingdom of Kósomos came to the plaza to see the soldiers working, the Priest stood upon the balcony of King Urikiru's Palace and made this proclamation: "On the longest night of Winter when all the stars that shine in heaven have found the same position as the stars that shine inside the Palace dome, we will consecrate the Altar of the Spirit of the Dragon Who Dwells Within the Mountain. I here decree, that on that night every virgin girl in all the world must dance before the altar of the Dragon. When we find the blessed one whose grace is sweet enough to make the Spirit of the Dragon sing, she will be a very lucky child indeed." Skalyya raised his sacrificial knife and let it glisten in the sun. A frightened hush went through the crowd, but now the Priest spoke words of comfort: "For those who can see the world beyond, death is no more than a trifle. This child will live in paradise, and her mother and her father will know unknown riches here on earth." The Priest's proclamation was greeted at first with a brief silence, and then a tumultuous cheer.

All over the Kingdom, mothers and fathers started training their young daughters for the day when they would dance upon the Altar of the Spirit of the Dragon Who Dwells Within the Mountain. Meanwhile, Skalyya, determined that every human soul should play a part within his pageant, kept watch from the parapets of the King's Palace. His eye scanned the distant forests and meadows for any sign of the wily girl who was rumored to live in the wilderness, far beyond the high walls of Kósomos.

Far over the horizon, Ololo rested after a long night of flying from branch to branch. Even from this distance, he could hear the faint rumble of the stones that the King's soldiers were rolling into the plaza, the whine and wail of the Priest's proclamation, and the frenzied cheers that followed it. He knew that something wicked was afoot, though he could not guess just what it was. Thoroughly exhausted, he fell asleep at the top of his tree and dreamt again that he was drinking his mother's warm milk and hiding in the darkness of her hair. He listened to the music of the birds in the trees all around him and remembered the words that his mother has whispered to him, first in one ear and then in the other.

Ololo awoke with the sun in his eyes and his mother nowhere to be seen. His belly was empty and ached with hunger. He looked down through the branches and saw a meadow where a feast grew from the earth, waiting to be harvested. He saw clusters of bright berries spread like stars among the bushes, long bananas as brilliant as the sun hanging below mangoes as dark and full of color as the twilight sky. He was about to climb down to harvest the fruit, when he noticed something else: this garden was full of tigers, sleeping in the underbrush. There was not a single speck of fruit inside that garden that was not within the striking distance of a deadly cat.

The Monkey grew delirious with hunger as his gaze swung back and forth between the tigers and the feast of fruit, and he waited for the cats to leave. Ololo discovered that tigers are lazy and can sleep for an eternity. He was nearly asleep himself when he saw a group of golden apes with bright red rumps come traipsing through the tall grass towards the fragrance of the hanging fruit. The smallest of the tribe stepped on a big cat's tail. The tiger stood and roared at them with all the anger of a beast whose morning nap has been broken. The group of apes stood paralyzed. The wee one let out a frightened squeak, but no one dared to help her. The Monkey put an arrow in his bow.

The musical twang of the Monkey's golden bow echoed

through the wilderness as an arrow flew across the sky and snapped a branch that held a beehive high above the meadow. When the beehive landed on a fragile bough of leaves just above the largest tiger's head, a cloud of furious bees emerged. Ololo played a curious tune on his bow and the bees set to work attacking the cats. Soon the whole streak of tigers ran off across the riverbend, as fast as if they were on fire. Now safe from both small bees and giant cats, the young ape squeaked once and scrambled into the arms of her mother.

When they saw that the great tigers were gone, the blond apes rejoiced and swarmed into the mango grove to harvest up its fruit. Before any ape bit into a succulent mango, though, the Old Ape who led the tribe squeaked and grunted again and commanded the others to place a pile of mangoes, bananas, and hibiscus flowers at the base of the tree whence the golden arrow had come. "We must thank our protector," the old ape declared, "before we feed ourselves." He retrieved the golden arrow that had split the beehive and set it, with great care, atop the offering. Ololo kept himself hidden behind the branches until the apes had feasted and sung their after-dinner songs and gone to sleep. Then, when he was sure that he would perish from hunger if he waited any longer, he came down to eat the pile of fruit and flowers that they had left for him.

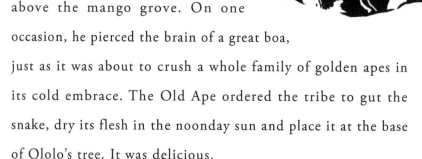

The strange songs the Old Ape sang to soothe his tribe each night became the food of Ololo's dreams. The days and months passed, and the Monkey grew fatter and never found a reason, being so good with his bow and arrow, to leave his tree high above the mango grove. On one occasion, he pierced the brain of a great boa, just as it was about to crush a whole family of golden apes in its cold embrace. The Old Ape ordered the tribe to gut the snake, dry its flesh in the noonday sun and place it at the base of Ololo's tree. It was delicious.

On another evening that he would never forget, as the horizon rose in the west to swallow the sun, Ololo rescued the ancient sage and leader of the tribe. The Old Ape had such a strong smell and moved so slowly that he was often mistaken for dead by the scavengers in the sky. While he was engrossed in his studies and prayers, a powerful red-headed vulture who had been circling the grove swooped down to pick him up with his talons. As the Old Ape rose in the air, Ololo trained his arrow on the bird's bright gizzard. The sage, who was hanging terrified in the air, looked straight into the Monkey's eyes just as he let his arrow fly. The bird lost its head, and the arrow flew far into the wilderness. As the Old Ape fell from this great height, the other apes hurried to catch him. When they asked the Old Ape if he had seen the guardian and protector who lived up in the sky, he stuttered for a while before he managed to say, "Yes, I saw Him. But He is beyond the power of words to describe." The other apes were puzzled for a while because the Old Ape had never in his life been at a loss for words, but no one dared to ask him more about what he had seen.

The animals in the forest must have some way to tell each other about a common danger, because it wasn't long before the music of Ololo's bow was enough to scare off the hungry cats, snakes, vultures and other predators from the happy garden where the red-bottomed apes now made their home. With his skill and vigilance, Ololo had made the Mango Grove into a garden where the tribe of golden apes could live and thrive in peace.

After he had finished eating his supper each night, Ololo liked to lie back in his perch under the moon and stars and gaze at the city on the back of the coin. He admired its concentric streets and radiating avenues and the three strong walls around it. On the other side of the coin, Ololo studied the archer who stood atop a cloud and protected the city down below. He knew that he was looking at himself. Ololo heard a voice that was like his own but older, and a little weary. This voice had spoken to him again and again before he was born, and now he recalled its soothing recitation. "You will keep the people safe and spare them from destruction."

One morning while Ololo was admiring his image on the front of the coin, he dropped his medallion and heard it fall from branch to branch, until it landed at the base of his tree. There the Old Ape picked it up and his buttocks flamed blood red with excitement. "This is a sign from heaven! This is the archer who lives up in the sky and protects us all! This is his gift to us!" The whole tribe of apes gathered round to see at last a picture of the archer whom the Old Ape had been unable to describe.

On hearing the commotion at the base of his tree, Ololo climbed down and addressed the crowd of ecstatic blond apes who had gathered there. Ololo declared, "Yes, I am the archer in the sky who protects you. But that medallion is not a gift. I merely dropped it by mistake and would like to have it back."

At this the apes fell into a riot of laughter that frightened all the songbirds away. When they stopped to catch their breath, it was silent in the forest. "I am the archer who protects you.

Why do you laugh at me?" And then the whole tribe of golden apes laughed again, while the Old Ape laughed the loudest and pointed his long and mangy finger at Ololo. When he caught his breath and was able to speak again, he clapped his hands with great authority and a pair of nimble apes snatched away Ololo's hunting bow and his quiver of arrows. "You are more than a common monkey, my friend, to make us laugh so well. But you are not the archer who lives up in the sky. His picture is here for all to see on this medallion" The Old Ape held up the coin and the others bowed their heads before it.

Furious at their stupidity, and at the Old Ape's lie, Ololo jumped on the ancient ape and tried to take his gold medallion back. This proved to be impossible as the Old Ape's grip was as stiff as rigor mortis and Ololo was unwilling to hurt such an ancient creature. He wrestled for a long time with the younger apes and won back his bow and just two of his arrows. A gang of tiny apes ran off into the underbrush with the remaining nine, but Ololo did not bother to chase them. He spoke with all the dignity that he could muster to the mocking congregation of red-bottomed apes, "Keep the other arrows to remember me by. And may the gold medallion that bears my likeness serve to protect you all when the tigers return, because I will be long gone."

Determined to get as far as he could from the ungrateful tribe of apes, and to reach the golden city on the coin where he was destined to be King, Ololo leapt from tree to tree long past nightfall until he came to a river that was too wide to cross. Ololo sat back and did what he had done on every night that he had spent in the wilderness: He listened to the news from the birds all around and learned whatever it had to teach him about the whole wide world.

After Ololo had listened for several nights an Owl came to him and told him this story:

I used to live in the body of a man. My hands could hold tools that cut stone, and I loved to make beautiful things for people to touch and admire. Guided by a slow and gentle music behind my eyes, I cut tiles of every size and shape and color that fit together and made music before my eyes. No two tiles I made were alike, but each tile had one place where it would fit as smooth as a song.

I loved cutting these tiles and people from all around loved to piece them together even though it took some time. But then one day a strange man came to me. He looked straight at me and said, "I have no time." This was a puzzle to me, because I had never met someone who had no time. So I asked him why. He showed me a hammer as big as my head and answered,

"Because I have this." Then he threw some coins on the ground and called a team of men to join him. They took all my tools and every tile that I had ever made and carted them away to his palace. Day and night, I would hear him cursing and striking with his hammer, and I could hear my tiles crack and splinter and split as he jammed them into place.

I climbed the mountain above his palace and saw him working without stopping, by sunlight and torchlight, on his powerful design. His men bowed to him and, when he asked (which was often) they told him it was a brilliant picture and that he was the greatest artist who had ever hammered tiles into place. Seeing they were right, in their way, I lost all desire to hold my tools again and leapt from that mountain. By some grace that I did not think to ask for, I became the stone-colored owl that I am today. All my designs are memories and all my memories are songs. Hoo. Hoooo. Hoooooo.

The Owl flew away.

The Owl's story made Ololo feel lonely, and every time
heard it *hoo* in the distance, his loneliness grew deeper and
wider. Days passed and he hoped all the while to hear the voice
that he had heard on the night of his escape from the Assassin
and the Secretary. The moon was full above, and Ololo saw
another moon in the center of the river and thought that the
river must be very deep to hold another sky inside it. Across
the river, he saw a quiet dark-haired girl pick up a dandelion
and blow its seeds across the water. Lit by moons from above
and below, the seeds were not hard to see, and Ololo hoped at
least one would make it all the way across the river. Without
thinking once about it, he played a little tune on his bow to
help the seed across.

Hearing the music from Ololo's bow, Tahualamne stood up
and looked for him in the branches of the tree, but she could
not see him. One seed from her dandelion managed to cross
over to the far bank, and as Ololo continued to play, she danced
to his music to show how glad she was.

All night he plucked the single string with all ten fingers
and all ten toes and made new sounds no soul has ever made
before or since, and Tahualamne danced as if to pull the music
out of him.

Meanwhile, deep in the forest behind Tahualamne, the Priest cut through the branches with his knife. He was determined to have every virgin girl in the world play a part in his fantastic pageant before the Altar of the Spirit of the Dragon, and now he set out looking for the wily girl rumored to live in the wilderness.

The Priest, who was a stout little man, coveted beautiful things more than any soul on earth. While the King battled the Dragon, Skalyya studied the creature's form and motion with great care. In deference to the ancient warnings, he dared not look into her eyes, but memorized the grace of her limbs and the curious pattern of her scales. He made certain that the Altar of the Spirit of the Dragon that the King's men had built in the plaza was magnificent and accurate in each detail. The same was true for the miraculous gift that he had made to please the King and earn his loyalty. Over the years, the King grew obsessed with perfecting Kósomos, and began to ignore his Queen. Skalyya never stopped admiring her radiance and noble grace, though he dared not speak to her. He watched her from afar and memorized every detail of her form and grace. This silent shell that Skalyya had created for the King was more than a trick of magic; she was animated by his secret longings and made from his blood and hair and carefully distilled secretions.

The strange and beautiful music of Ololo's bow drew him to the riverside. When he saw Tahualamne dancing beneath the moon he was nearly paralyzed by the sight of her, but his admiration of her beauty was not as strong as his will to possess it. As she spun to the rhythm of Ololo's fugue, the old Priest held his breath, tread quietly and grabbed her from behind. She let out a cry that Ololo recognized immediately from the night that she had saved his life. He stood helpless on his side of the river as the Priest wrapped her at once in his dark black cloak, covered her mouth with his pale sweaty hand, and carried her off into the darkness.

Ololo darted forward to rescue her. He scrambled over a long tree branch that stretched halfway across the river to see if he could leap across. The branch bent under his weight, which had grown from all the mangoes eaten during his reign as the protector of the red-bottomed apes. The wood creaked and threatened to snap just above the water. Below, on the dark and glassy surface of the river, he saw a hairy monkey surrounded by the moon and stars looking back at him. It was the same awful creature that had chased him into the darkness of Rakelvor's bag. In a panic, Ololo scurried to escape the sight, but the branch gave way. He looked down in horror as he saw the hairy monkey extend its arms and pull him straight into the water.

The hairy creature wrestled with Ololo in the current until he didn't know which way was up or down. When he finally got his head above the water, he saw that he was caught in a whirlpool, heading toward a giant chasm that swallowed all the water in the river and filled the valley all around it with a deafening white noise.

Sure that he was about to die, he could only think about Tahualamne and the cold eyes of the man in the black cloak who had taken her away.

TAHUALAMNE

You will never remember how to spell
Her name, or the way her face
Shines in the dusk, or even tell

If what lingers in your eye's a trace
Of something real, or just a thing
You hoped and hope for. The place

And time are sunk in the flood. Nothing
Happened you can be sure. The one
Who taught your bow at once to sing

That one is gone

Ololo was sucked into the vortex of falling water, then churned out into a place where everything was dark. The water was still, and the smell and heat of rottenness locked itself around his senses. There were no stars or flowers or sweet and dusky mangoes here. There was no climbing or leaping from tree to tree. He lay on his back and drifted with the current until the only sounds he heard were drops of water that came down from invisible cracks in the ceiling and the rats that scratched and prodded and squeaked.

The Monkey had seen things die before and be eaten by the wilderness. Once he saw a carcass so covered with flies that their thick black bodies and prismatic wings eclipsed its form as the manic noise of their appetites drowned out all the other sounds in the forest. The Monkey figured that he must be dead now, and this suffocating darkness must be what it was like on the underside of that blanket of flies.

As he drifted farther down the dark canal, he came to a spot where some light seemed to leak from around the corner. Now he could make out the banks of the canal and saw some skeletons strewn about. Some skulls grinned back at him, still others had lost their lower jaws, and the rest were smashed apart like the plates he had broken in the King's Palace on the night that he was born.

In a far corner, Ololo saw the blue silk gown his mother wore on the evening she suckled him and poured her life into his blood. The blue was still deep enough for his eyes to swim in, but it was torn into pieces that lay scattered on the floor. He saw a skull beside the gown with the same teeth that once nibbled his ear. She seemed to look back at him from the darkness of her eyes, and Ololo thought he felt her presence. Suddenly, the skull began to move, as if it were about to speak to him. A fat rat crawled out from behind the skull and looked into the Monkey's eyes. As it turned away to crawl off into the darkness its tail brushed an object. The Monkey heard the sound of glass against stone and saw a familiar shape that glistened even in the dimmest light. He could not, though his throat tightened to see it now, leave the obsidian dagger. His mother had stood in the path of its flight to save his life, but his father had meant it for him. And now it had found him here. He picked up the King's oldest weapon, still sharp enough to cut his fingers, and tossed it in the quiver on his back.

The Monkey kept moving. He paddled through the darkness, until around another bend, he was blinded by a shaft of sunlight that came down through a column from straight above him. He put his hands and feet on the smooth stone walls of the column and pulled himself up out of the filthy water. When he looked down, he saw the hairy beast raise his tail mockingly and flaunt his buttocks, surrounded by what looked like a halo of sunlight. A pale alligator swam in slow circles around the wretched thing and glared up at Ololo. He recoiled, then turned his eyes to the sky and climbed as fast as he could.

Soon Ololo could no longer see the bottom of the chasm, and his ears began to pop, for he was higher than any tree that he had ever seen in the forest. The light coming from above steadily dimmed. Ololo kept climbing toward the fading light, until a white flash lit the chasm, followed by the sound of thunder breaking in the distance. Soon, a trickle and then a torrent of rainwater washed down over him. To keep from falling, he had to press the walls so tight that his fingers nearly bled, but Ololo was glad to be washed clean by the rush of rain.

The rain stopped. Soon the light of the moon poured

into the chasm, and the Monkey resumed his ascent. When he could climb no higher, he found a large iron grate directly above him. He pushed and shoved at the grate until it loosened enough for him to slip through. Ololo pulled himself up into an enormous room with five strange windows open to the night sky and the wind. The largest of these angled downward like a grimace and was lined on the top and bottom with rows of sharp stone teeth. Above this long and crooked crescent gate he saw a pair of smaller holes that let in the cool breeze, and above those were two large oval openings that gazed up at the stars. The wind whistled all around him and made the chasm underneath him rumble the way an empty bottle answers a steady rush of air. Ololo felt certain that he was now inside a living thing, though he could not say what it was.

Ololo looked down at the city to admire how coolly it shone in the light of the night sky. Tonight, he could not see as many stars in the sky, and the moon, though full, seemed somehow not to be as bright. Ololo looked to the window with the jagged teeth around it and saw a world of dancing yellow lights come to life below.

He crouched between two stone teeth and looked down,

and Ololo saw the city he had admired so many times on the gold face of his lost medallion now spread out before him, a thousand times larger than he had ever dreamt. While the coin had only glowed with borrowed light, the city down below seemed to be made of light itself, and populated by a race of walking, murmuring stars. Unlike the stars in the sky, which seemed to be scattered with no clear design, these points of light flowed through radiating boulevards toward a common center. When all the stars had gathered in the plaza below Ololo's perch, he wept to see a thing so beautiful, and wished that the girl who had danced to his music across the river were also there to see it.

When all the people of the Kingdom of Kósomos had gathered in the plaza, Ololo saw the stout little man in the long black robe who had taken Tahualamne away the night before. His eyes focused on the long knife in the little man's hand. The Priest raised his knife in the air and announced that the ceremony would begin. Ololo looked down as King Urikiru knelt in the plaza far below him, kissed the ground and begged for forgiveness. "Oh, great Spirit of the Dragon, I know I have offended thee, and thou hast rightly cursed me by denying me an heir. And yet the good people of this realm deserve a King to guide them and protect them after I have died. Tonight, we will select the fairest virgin child who most pleases you and pour her blood into your fire as a humble offering to your great spirit, in the hope that you will smile upon our kingdom and bless us with a healthy heir." And with these words the King rubbed the belly of his pregnant Queen. She looked to all the world like the great and beautiful Queen Ambu, and all the world called her that, but Ololo saw her pale, empty eyes and knew that she was not.

As the King and Queen sat down, Skalyya bowed his head and said a prayer that not a soul could comprehend, and the pageant had begun. A single drum began to play, and one after the other, every young girl in the Kingdom came and danced upon the Altar of the Dragon Who Dwells Within the Mountain, as the people watched in reverent silence. Every single dancing girl cast a nervous glance upward, straight at the spot where Ololo now sat alone in the darkness of the Dragon's head. The girls all seemed terrified, but the dances they danced were marvelous and well-rehearsed in each detail. The whole pageant was pleasing to the eyes and ears of Ololo, but it filled his heart with sadness. He could only think of Tahualamne and how she had danced just as she pleased for him, beneath the moon beside the flowing river.

When the ninety-eighth girl had finished her dance, the drumbeat stopped, and a terrible silence fell over the Kingdom. The great stone Dragon had not given the people a sign. It seemed that no one in the pageant had shown grace enough to please the Spirit of the Dragon Who Dwells Within the Mountain. A murmur spread through the crowd until the Priest commanded, "Silence! The pageant is not finished yet. Just as I commanded, *every* virgin girl on the vast island of the world must dance before the Altar of the Spirit of the Dragon. I now present to you Tahualamne, the wild child who has always lived outside the walls of our Kingdom." The Priest pulled aside a sheet of black silk and revealed to all a simple cage with Tahualamne inside it. When he opened the cage and Tahualamne stepped out, the people of the Kingdom roared with laughter. Every girl in the pageant had been a picture of poise and grace, and none of them had pleased the Dragon. Here was a girl with dark matted hair, tawny skin, strong hands, and large, calloused feet! How could she be pleasing to the wise and ancient spirit of the Dragon?

Ololo knew better. When she stood upon the Altar, his eyes drank in her grace. Kósomos, in all of its magnificence, seemed to disappear and he was back beside the river. With all ten fingers and all ten toes, the Monkey plucked his bow and began again the symphony that he had played the night before. Now it echoed from within the darkness of the Dragon's head and each note was as loud as thunder and as sweet as rain. Tahualamne, thrilled to know that he was near, performed a dance for him so graceful and so true it silenced the crowd and humbled every soul within the Kingdom who had laughed at her.

Even Skalyya, whose eyes were as cold and sharp as his sacrificial knife, wept openly to see Tahualamne dance. "She is the one!" He declared and showed the world his pale hand as he wiped his tears away. "Her grace has made the Dragon sing! She is the one!"

And with these words, Skalyya raised up his sacrificial knife for all to see. He ran its edge along a spinning wheel and a stream of magic sparks flew across the plaza. The people gasped in awe at such a miracle. As all the children of the Kingdom stood up to get a better look, Skalyya poured in Tahualamne's ear a mixture of juices so noxious that the Monkey could smell its powerful fumes from high above the plaza. As she collapsed, two soldiers came and placed her on a bed of flowers.

His eye now locked on the Priest, Ololo quietly placed an arrow in his bow.

The Priest lit a fire on the Altar of the Spirit of the Dragon Who Dwells Within the Mountain and held his knife above her neck. "You have been chosen above all the others. We pour your blood into the fire to feed the Spirit of the Dragon who Dwells Within the Mountain," he declared in somber tones, and the people of the Kingdom closed their eyes and repeated every word he said.

The Monkey let his arrow fly. It struck near the hilt of Skalyya's knife and sent it tumbling from his panicked hand into the fire. When the people heard the twang of Ololo's bow they thought the stone Dragon had spoken again. Every eye looked up at the altar as the Priest reached into the fire to retrieve his sacrificial knife. The Monkey played a wily tune that made the old Priest lose his footing.

On the altar where he had planned to sacrifice Tahualamne, the Priest now gave himself to the fire. He sputtered and exploded like hot grease. His body yielded a noxious black smoke that reeked of elephant dung, congealed fat, and sulfur. Across the plaza the Priest's creation, who looked to all the world like the great and beautiful Ambu, burst into a flash of flame that settled as a pile of smoking ash beside the startled King. The noxious smoke of the Priest floated far beyond the walls of the Kingdom. It climbed the steep side of the black mountain, passed over strange and misshapen rocks, and slipped into the blind and bottomless cave where the Dragon slept. It curled in the Dragon's nostrils and entered the kingdom of her dreams like a small seed drifting over the walls of a fortified city.

THE DRAGON

A dragon sleeping in her nest
Draws new iron from old rust
She will stay and drink her rest

Another eon if she must
Do not wake her to enquire
If her dreams are wise or just

Tonight, a king drunk with desire
And torn from peace by anger's claw
Will summon her into his fire

As she wraps him in her law

The smoke of Skalyya's flesh seeped into the Dragon's mind and woke up all her injuries. She felt the stub of her tail, the empty wound where her right eye had been, her wounded foot, and the mark that the King had cut into her chest. She dreamt of a broken wall, a great fire, and a river of blood. This time she would eat every soul in the Kingdom and flatten every home. She would extinguish every light, and the stars would shine more brightly when she was done.

And this time, she thought, they would not see her coming. As the Dragon burrowed through the earth toward the kingdom, the valley buckled and shook with so much force that the world itself seemed like it would split in half. The walls of Kósomos rattled and shifted on their foundations and the gates of the city twisted and squeaked in their jambs. The outer gates of the city broke open, and the well-tended animals of Kósomos, the pigs, goats and elephants, even the silkworms and the honeybees, all fled toward the wilderness. Only the people remained, locked in by the strongest and innermost gate.

As the people, fearing as the earth kept shaking that the kingdom would collapse upon them, gathered at the gate and cried out for the King to open it, Urikiru stood before them and blocked their path. "I built this Kingdom as a refuge to protect you all. Life and light are safe within these walls. Only death and darkness lie without. I am your guardian and your King, and I forbid you to leave."

The earth shuddered and bolted, and the people cried out again for the King to open up the gate. In answer to their pleas, the Monkey took his last arrow and placed it in his bow. He drew his bowstring back as far as it would go and let the arrow fly. It was as if the rusty lock had been waiting for eternity to be pierced by the Monkey's aim. The musical twang of Ololo's bow echoed from the capacious stone Dragon's head as though a god had spoken, and with a slow and grating creak, the gate swung open behind Urikiru. The King cursed and spat, while the people cheered and thanked the spirit of the Dragon.

The gate was open. The path of escape was clear. Yet no one stepped forward to defy the King.

"If you break my command," declared the King, "you end your own lives." Two of the King's guards quietly drew their swords and tried to sneak behind their master. The King was old and held no weapons but proved again he was no one to be trifled with. When the first guard tried to stab the King in his back, Urikiru flipped him over and impaled him on his own sword. He then swung around, grabbed the sword of the second man and calmly as a butcher in the marketplace, cut the tendons of his heels with one stroke. He then advised the soldier: "You are free to go now. The door is open. Crawl off into the wild if it suits you." As the wounded man twisted on the ground behind Urikiru, the earth beneath Kósomos continued to shudder and creak, and others came at the King, in groups of three and four and five with shields and spears and swinging chains.

Armed only with a single iron sword, Urikiru fought more

fiercely than he had fought against the Dragon. Disobedience was more hateful to him than any monster in the wilderness. The King was ten times the warrior of his strongest soldier. He alone had tamed the wilderness around Kósomos and gathered the stones to build its walls. His people were merely to tend the haven that he had created.

The soldiers were younger and stronger than the King, but Urikiru was adept at using their own force against them. He studied each advance and dodged each blow at exactly the right instant. His reflexes were as lethal and sharp as they had ever been, and though he was wounded many times in this fight, he never faltered. The earth continued to tremble and rock, and the bodies of soldiers fell around Urikiru's feet like acorns around a broad oak tree when it is shaken by the wind.

As her claws widened the ancient caves far beneath the city, the Dragon licked her teeth clean and snorted, dreaming that the blood of the people of Kósomos was flowing like a river into the cleansing fire of her gut. As she fed the fire in her chest, she also wept with joy at the thought of a world without mankind, where the only light at night would be the light of the moon and stars and the only speech heard in the valley would be from the congress of the birds. These thoughts and visions sped her purpose, and soon she was beneath the very center of the kingdom.

The Dragon pushed upward until she found herself beneath a starlit sky, bathing in a cool and quiet sea. She breathed the perfume from the flowers gathered on the Island of the World, and her scales, washed glistening clean by an ocean without tides, traded light with the golden constellations of stars that seemed close enough to touch. She studied the green Island of the World, and the great black mountain that was her home. The three walls and the white dome of Kósomos were nowhere to be seen. The Dragon was shocked. The world was still a perfect secret and mankind had never been.

The Dragon spent a long moment basking in the joy of a world without mankind and admiring its beauty, until her tail, or the stump of it, brushed lightly against the dome of stars above her head. The dream was over. These were not the distant fires in the sky, but pictures on the ceiling of a cave a thousand times smaller than her capacious lair inside the great black mountain.

She felt at once that she was suffocating, and a memory came back to her that she could not name or explain. There was an instant she had endured eons before when the only world she had known, and world that had nurtured and created her, had suddenly become a trap, a place that would become her grave if she did not break out of it and see what was beyond. As if her muscles had their own memory, the Dragon shifted inside the

Palace Dome, and began to push with all her strength against the sky of gilded stars.

When no soldiers were left to defy him, Urikiru stood with a litter of broken bodies at his feet and glared back at his people. He dropped the broken sword in his hand and the sound of its iron against stone now echoed through the Kingdom of Kósomos. The King, wounded and unarmed, was now the only obstacle between the people and the wilderness, but he was more confident than ever that none of them would dare defy him now.

After a long moment of silence, the King addressed his people. "The danger is passed. Gather these broken weapons together and take them to the ironworks. We will forge three new iron gates for the kingdom of Kosó—"

The King was interrupted by an enormous cracking sound from the center of Kósomos. Behind the crowd of people, the Palace Dome broke open like an egg and the Dragon emerged, breathing a sigh of gratitude to taste the open air and see the real stars again. As she pushed her way out, the dome collapsed and shattered chunks of masonry, inlaid with lapis and golden stars came crashing down around the plaza.

Their terror of the living Dragon made the people of Kósomos brave enough to defy the King. They surged forward in an instant and trampled King Urikiru beneath ten thousand panicked feet. As they fanned out into the wilderness, carrying their lanterns and torches, the Dragon looked down at the specks of light that scattered outward from the Kingdom like the seeds of a dandelion. They spread in all directions, and the Dragon—who had sworn that she would kill them all—now knew that their race would grow and thrive and inhabit every corner of the world. Her cry of anguish was deep and guttural, and scared the people so that they ran even faster in all directions, far into the night.

The King, who had built such mighty walls to keep his people safe, was now part of his Kingdom, pounded into the plaza by the traffic of ten thousand feet.

Inside the empty cavern of the stone Dragon's head, the Monkey remembered a voice full of hope and kindness that had spoken to him on many nights before he was born: *You will keep the people safe and spare them from destruction.* Ololo, born to be the King of Kósomos, now wept for the King, his father.

He looked down at Tahualamne where she slept and saw that the deafening noise of the Dragon breaking through the Palace dome, though it shook the fruit from the trees and rattled every paving stone, was not enough to wake her. Ololo feared that she was dead, but he could now see the color in her cheeks and the slow undulation of her breathing.

The Dragon lowered her eyes and sniffed at the spot where the King had been trampled. A Dragon's face is hard to read, but Ololo thought that he could see a smile there. Whatever the feeling was, it didn't last long. The Dragon turned her maw and nostrils up toward heaven and let out a lonely whimper and looked up at the stars, and the full moon rising over the mountainside.

Then she squatted down on her big haunches and blew out every torch and candle in the city. At last when she blew out the sacrificial fire in which the Priest had perished, the moon shone down on everything, and soaked into its walls and streets until the ruined city was glowing from the inside out.

The Dragon looked down on Tahualamne atop her altar and whispered a long series of sounds, all of them as distinct as words though none of them familiar, into her sleeping ear. Tahualamne smiled in her sleep, but she did not awaken.

The creature stood up to her full height and looked straight at the stone Dragon that Ololo was hiding inside. Few souls in the history of the earth have ever seen a Dragon weep, but the Monkey did that night. The Dragon, with her stub of a tail, rotten left foot, and wound in her side, now wept from her one good eye to see her mortal form as it had once been.

Now the Dragon took a closer look at her glorious form and saw the Monkey inside her head. Ololo looked back at the Dragon and, though he was almost too terrified to move, he reached into his quiver and pulled out the obsidian dagger.

She looked up at heaven and wondered how such things could be. Not only did this jeweled tower of stone resemble her in every way, but it revealed her own thoughts, as they had been on the day that she had battled the King. The Dragon remembered how, as she dragged herself back to her cave, she'd cast a curse upon the King: "May his first-born son and only heir be born a monkey." And here the Monkey stood, inside her own head, just as she'd imagined him.

His breathing slowed and his eyesight sharpened as Ololo raised the obsidian dagger behind his head. The old Dragon grinned and let out a low reptilian wheeze that was her way of laughing. Sensing that the giant creature was no longer angry— at least not at this moment—Ololo relaxed but kept the dagger behind his head, ready to send it flying.

As the Dragon continued to laugh and weep, her eye became a vortex of colors and forms that turned with a slow and dizzying power. Ololo tried to look away, but just as the whirlpool had pulled him in from the river's edge, the spiral storm inside the Dragon's eye drew him in against his will. Here was everything. He saw the dark interlocking leaves of the forest canopy, so green that they were almost black, the silver mirror scales of the fish that swim in circles in the eddies of the river, and the birds with iridescent feathers that trace endless circles in the sky. The music of the birds was here though not as sound but as a thread of light that wove its way through every shape in radiating undulations. Ololo even saw the current of magma that flows miles below the city and the river of stars that flows across the night sky above. He saw the yellow bee and the blue dragonfly, the slow green kiss of the snail on the granite stone beneath the red hibiscus tree and the spiral of its shell.

In the center of this vortex, though, the Monkey saw something that alarmed and disgusted him and made him ready to use the weapon in his hand. In the deep black canoe of the Dragon's pupil, he saw the selfsame hairy ape who had chased him into Rakelvor's bag, pulled him into the river, and thrown him into the whirlpool. Now the beast held a dagger cocked behind his head and threatened to send it flying straight into Ololo's heart.

The two of them sat motionless for a long time, the colors of the Dragon's eye in slow orbit all around them, until Ololo determined that he would throw first. He aimed straight at the Monkey's heart and sent his father's obsidian dagger whistling through the air. As he watched the dagger fly, he saw the pupil of the Dragon's eye narrow with fear and all the colors disappear from its iris. Every living thing that Ololo saw within the Dragon's eye began to wither and die as soon as the blade took flight. The music of the birds was broken and the luminous thread went dark.

Ololo screeched in despair, but immediately fell silent when he saw what happened next. The Archer whose face and form he knew from the golden coin stood calmly in the center of the Dragon's eye where the hairy ape had been. The man stood with his arms at his side and stared at the dagger. It stopped in the middle of the air just so long as the Archer from the medallion kept his eyes fixed upon its blade. The Archer lifted his eyes to look straight into Ololo's eyes. He smiled as the dagger flew and pierced his flesh, as though he did not feel a thing. The color returned to the Dragon's eye and the spiraling wheel of birds and skies and fish and streams and flowers and boughs of trembling leaves resumed their living orbit around the deep black pupil.

Ololo stood and admired the noble Prince inside the Dragon's eye and stepped closer to see him better. But as the sun broke over the distant mountains, the image of the serene Prince inside the Dragon's eye was nowhere to be seen. Suddenly, he doubled over in agony and felt the obsidian dagger buried in his chest. Its glass blade had come closer than the width of an ant's antenna to rupturing his heart, before it stopped. Just as the King's bowl had overflowed with deep red wine on the night that he was born, Ololo felt an ecstasy of pain, as ancient as the Dragon's blood, pour into him and overflow. A darkness deeper than Rakelvor's black silk bag wrapped itself around him and his thoughts fled in all directions the way that the people had fled the city last night in their terror of the Dragon.

He felt a violent blast of wind rush over his body. The dragon had two eyes again, and they looked straight into his. She had earned her wings and was now a great flying beast with iridescent black feathers that flashed violet in the sun. She had a graceful long neck, like a young and hungry cormorant. The feathered serpent circled the city and all the people who had fled Kósomos could see it from every corner of the valley. The living Dragon, in its new form, perched on the shoulders of the stone dragon and stuck its head inside to speak to Ololo in the language of the birds.

"Little man! Do you want me to pull that dagger from your chest and drop it off the edge of earth?" she enquired.

"Yes." said Ololo in the language of the birds.

The bird closed its long bill around Ololo's left leg and pulled him out of the stone dragon's head. She flew him far from the city as she looked for the edge of the earth and showed him everything that he had seen inside the Dragon's eye in the world around him. He still felt the pain of the obsidian blade in his chest, but as he dangled upside down from the feathered serpent's beak he felt the cool rush of the air over his body,

and his senses were flooded with a new sort of life by the sights
and sounds around him. She flew
him over forests screeching
with birds, mountains
jagged and soft with
snow, deserts where
the wind writes its
name in the sand,
and far out over the
boundless sea where
the wind writes its name
in the water. She flew him across the day side of the world and
through the night side of the world and out the other side of
night into the day. There was no edge of the world from which
to drop the knife, so they returned to the Kingdom of Kósomos.
She carried him high above the city and let go of his leg to
pluck the dagger from his chest and cast it down. The dagger
plummeted through the air and Ololo fell fast behind it. He
tumbled towards the plaza in the center of the city and heard
the air rushing in his ears as he picked up speed. He heard the
obsidian dagger shatter on the stones just beneath him, and,
just as he was expecting to die, the great flying creature grabbed
his leg in her bill and swooped him up again. The great bird
set Ololo down in the center of the plaza next to Tahualumne.
Ololo felt the wind of its wings as it rose in the air above him,

and he looked up to see this single feathered serpent break apart into ten thousand different birds of every size, shape, and color. These birds flew in cacophonous funnel cloud, high into the sky, but soon their songs merged into a curious harmony that grew fainter with their growing distance from the ground. They circled a city in ruins, where the only structure standing was a dragon made of stone. Finally the birds went their separate ways, and out to the horizon in all directions.

Ololo looked down at his chest. There was not a trace of blood. There was, however, a very distinct scar on Ololo's chest where the obsidian dagger had entered his body: the Seal of Kósomos, a bow and arrow (or was it a bird in flight?) identical to the scar that the King had left upon the Dragon's side. It was, he knew, a bird.

Tahualamne opened her eyes and rose to dance with Ololo. He was as sweet to her eyes as his song had been, and her dance was more enchanting to his soul than any song that he could play. Ololo and Tahualamne danced for a long while in the center of the plaza as the birds beyond the city wall made new music for them. Each of them became so lost in the other's eyes that neither noticed they were soon surrounded by a horde of dirty golden apes with bright red behinds.

THE GOLDEN APES

We wandered over thorny flats
Through mazes thickly twined
To flee the hungry snakes and cats

But no shelter did we find
Until an arrow from above
Saved the smallest of our kind

And brought peace to the mango grove
Where on that day we came to roam
Whilst whistling a song of love

We prayed would lead us home
Whilst whistling a song of love
We prayed would lead us home

When Ololo turned to look at them, the oldest of
the apes declared, "You are the archer who lives up in the sky
and protects us from above. I prayed that one day you would

show your countenance to us, and now the day has come!" And with those words, the apes bowed gracefully and laid all the rest of Ololo's arrows and his gold medallion at his feet. And then they all joined hands and sang the Song of the Golden Apes in their wobbly, screechy voices. Ololo, who had cursed them once, bit his tongue to keep back tears and laughter. He bowed in gratitude, kissed the Old Ape on the cheek and whispered in his ear, "Our eyes have met before." The Old Ape stumbled and his wrinkled bottom flushed red for a moment, but, remembering the importance of his high office, he quickly regained his composure. Then they gathered fruits and flowers and made a feast for Ololo and Tahualamne. All of them ate and drank and danced and laughed until the sun went down and the moon came up and reached the top of the sky and fell back below the city wall.

Just before dawn, Tahualamne woke Ololo and they tiptoed past the sleeping apes. Before they left the broken city gates, Ololo paused at the dark red spot before the ruins of the Palace Dome where Queen Ambu had fallen and laid a circle of stones around it.

When Ololo and Tahualamne came to the outer gate of the city, they heard a rustling in the trees. Ololo thought that it must be a tiger and was reaching for his arrow when

Tahualamne stopped him. He looked up and saw a great white horse with a deep black crescent moon on her back emerge from the darkness of the forest and came forward to kiss Ololo on the side of his face as though she'd known him all his life. Ololo and then Tahualamne climbed on Kalypso's back and rode off toward the vanishing stars in the west as the sun crept up through the trees behind them.

Near noon, the oldest of the red-bottomed apes awoke and found that Ololo and Tahualamne had disappeared. He found the circle of stones that Ololo had left near the spot where the great and beautiful Queen Ambu had fallen. Here he discovered a little yellow flower that had taken root in a gap between the paving stones. Its yellow petals shined and mirrored the sun in the center of the circle. "A little yellow flower surrounded by a circle of stones. It is a sign from the archer who lives up in the clouds! We will revere the little yellow flower for all time." And the others bowed their heads and swore that they would always heed his wisdom.

Kalypsyo carried Ololo and Tahualamne deep into the woods until she came to the spot beneath the tree where Thorn and Rakelvor had been eaten by the tigers. Tahualamne's figure eight of thorny vine still rested on the ground, though it was nearly hidden now by the grass that had grown up around it. Ololo dismounted at the spot and helped Tahualamne down. The morning sun dropped coins of light through the forest canopy and the sound of life was thick in the air.

For the first time, Tahualamne brought her face close to his and, as slowly as the morning sun steals the jewels of water that the night has placed on the strands of a spider web, she kissed him on the lips. Ololo closed his eyes. The kaleidoscope of living shapes that he had seen inside the dragon's eye the night before, enveloped him again as if to claim him. He felt the arrow pass through his heart and make the world disappear.

R.S. Deese

R. S. Deese is the author of *We Are Amphibians* (University of California Press, 2015), *Surf Music* (Pelekinesis, 2017), and *Climate Change and the Future of Democracy* (Springer, 2019). He teaches history at Boston University.

Chuck Wadey

Chuck Wadey is an illustrator and art director in the video game industry, having worked for Activision, Team Chaos, Zynga, and Monumental. He has a BFA in Illustration from Art Center College of Design.

112 Harvard Ave #65
Claremont, CA 91711 USA

pelekinesis@gmail.com
www.pelekinesis.com

Pelekinesis titles are available through Small Press Distribution, Baker & Taylor,
Ingram, Gardners, and directly from the publisher's website.

Lightning Source UK Ltd.
Milton Keynes UK
UKHW021959250522
403527UK00003B/103